For the lovers and the huggers of
the world (and one in particular), Rx
—R. B.

For all the Gails . . .
—N. S.

SIMON & SCHUSTER BOOKS FOR YOUNG READERS • An imprint of Simon & Schuster Children's Publishing Division • 1230 Avenue of the Americas, New York, New York 10020 • Text © 2021 by Rachel Bright • Illustration © 2021 by Nadia Shireen • Book design © 2021 by Simon & Schuster, Inc. • Originally published in Great Britain in 2021 by Simon & Schuster UK Ltd. • First US edition 2021 • All rights reserved, including the right of reproduction in whole or in part in any form. • SIMON & SCHUSTER BOOKS FOR YOUNG READERS and related marks are trademarks of Simon & Schuster, Inc. • For information about special discounts for bulk purchases, please contact Simon & Schuster Special Sales at 1-866-506-1949 or business@simonandschuster.com. • The Simon & Schuster Speakers Bureau can bring authors to your live event. For more information or to book an event, contact the Simon & Schuster Speakers Bureau at 1-866-248-3049 or visit our website at www.simonspeakers.com. • The text for this book was set in Century Expanded BT. • Manufactured in China • 0721 SUK • 2 4 6 8 10 9 7 5 3 1 • Library of Congress Cataloging-in-Publication Data • Names: Bright, Rachel, author. • Shireen, Nadia, illustrator. • Title: Slug in love / Rachel Bright ; illustrations by Nadia Shireen. • Description: First edition. • New York : A Paula Wiseman Book, Simon & Schuster Books for Young Readers, 2022. • Audience: Ages 4-8 • Audience: Grades 2-3 • Summary: Doug the slug is looking for a hug and soon finds there is a friend for everyone. • Identifiers: LCCN 2021007960 (print) • LCCN 2021007961 (ebook) • ISBN 9781665900461 (hardcover) • ISBN 9781665900478 (ebook) • Subjects: CYAC: Stories in rhyme. • Slugs (Mollusks)—Fiction. • Friendship—Fiction. • Humorous stories. • Classification: LCC PZ8.3.B7678 Sl 2022 (print) • LCC PZ8.3.B7678 (ebook) • DDC [E]—dc23 • LC record available at https://lccn.loc.gov/2021007960 • LC ebook record available at https://lccn.loc.gov/2021007961. • ISBN 9781665900461 • ISBN 9781665900478 (ebook)

Slug
in
love

RACHEL BRIGHT

illustrated by NADIA SHIREEN

A Paula Wiseman Book
Simon & Schuster Books for Young Readers
New York   London   Sydney   Toronto   New Delhi

There goes
Doug.

Doug is a **slug** . . .

who needs a hug.

Hey, Doug!

Need a hug?

Yep.

Doug is a **slug**
in need of a hug.

Not me.

Not you.

So on plods Doug . . .

poor **slug**.

But **wait!**

Here is a *snail*!

A *snail* called Gail.

SHE is grimy, slippy, squelchy, slimy.

SHE is icky,

mucky,

yucky,

sticky.

She's THE ONE for lonely Doug!
Doug the **slug**
who needs a hug.

A *snail* like Gail?
It cannot fail!

"Uhhh," says Doug.

"**NOOOOO!**" wails Gail.
It seems our master plan DID fail.

So on goes Doug,

our lonesome **slug,**

who's **never** going to get a hug. . . .

Oh, Doug.

But . . . you never know

how, when, or why

some love might just come
flying by.

This is Doug.
He found his **bug**,
and now he's super-duper snug.

This is Doug.
He got his hug.
He is a **slug** . . .

. . . a **slug** in love.